IN THE BONSAI GARDEN

In the Bonsai Garden

Padraig Rooney

RAVEN ARTS PRESS

In the Bonsai Garden
is first published in 1988 by
The Raven Arts Press
P.O. Box 1430
Finglas
Dublin 11
Ireland

ISBN 1 85186 032 0

Raven Arts Press receive financial assistance from The Arts
Council (An Chomhairle Ealaíon), Dublin, Ireland.

Designed by Dermot Bolger. Cover design by Susanne Linde.
Cover: detail from *The Spartan Boy* by Nathaniel Hone,
reproduced by kind permission of The National Gallery,
Dublin. Typeset and printed by Future Print in Dublin.

CONTENTS

I

IN THE BONSAI GARDEN

II PLACES

ACKNOWLEDGEMENTS

Acknowledgements are due to the following publications where some of these poems have previously appeared:

Aquarius, Beyond the Shore, Cyphers, An tEireannach, The Honest Ulsterman, Irish Press, Irish Times, Living in Thailand, The Nation (Bangkok), *North, Poetry Ireland Review.*

A selection of these poems appeared in *Raven Introductions 3*

This collection of poems won the Patrick Kavanagh Award for 1986.

In The Desert received a Special Commendation in the 1987 Arvon International Poetry Competition.

Grateful thanks are due to the Irish Arts Council (An Chomhairle Ealaíon) for its Bursary in Literature in 1984.

for my parents

IN THE BONSAI GARDEN

THE NATURAL HISTORY MUSEUM

The cold turnstiles creak with our passing out
from sunlight and the government buildings
— the glue-sniffers' convention we called it —
into the history of the species, the Darwin
chain unhooked by the free State employee,
and all its missing links, I among them.

We block the entrance like excursion kids
just up for the day from Monasterboyce
or Virginia, any provincial town.
My big-boned Dutch boy shines in the dark,
filling out the Continental denim
like taxidermy, all his tucks concealed.

I came here with my father years ago,
to see the lie of the land, its broad spectrum
from fossil to mammal, our chain of being.
Now with my son, the blond surrogate one
who's not on my passport, I catch me out
pointing and explaining, my father's role.

Who was it said we are poor forked creatures
risen from the slime? He leads me around
the showcases, all our banished reptiles,
the predatory birds, the small soft ones
he knows the names of in two languages
and cradled in the polders as a child.

I decipher the Latin roots, inked tags
fading behind the glass my boy mists up.
Their fixed habitats smell of old ether,
their eyes bright and hard as teddy bears'.
Our forked tongues move easily among them,
ornithologist, catcher in the rye.

All that moves is the 'thirties clock, ticking
our strange communion in this strange museum.
The noon sunlight comes through in blinding shafts
from the state buildings, the lie of the land.
We turnstile slowly back the way we came,
unhook the chain and vanish into light.

11

HIS WINTER LABORATORY

My father lived in winter laboratories,
unheated, where future experiments were stored.
The upper rooms of a Catholic seminary
held trays of cold birds' eggs, precious mercury.
He knew his natural science by heart,
the properties of stones, the laws which defied
the law of gravity. A fulcrum's breaking point.
His brain was a fertile hatchery.

Radium glowed in a special room beyond my reach,
scalpels for dissection in their velvet drawers.
His leather apron hung behind the door,
grey and flaccid, reeking of the tannery.
What failed discoveries hovered in the ether
which always stained his hands, I'll never know.
Caustic marks, lingering stigmata of an art
that moved and classified like a perfect surgeon.

The parts of animals, a chart of nature's tree
shone in snowy light above the bunsen burners.
An anatomy detailed, all its articulations known.
His oven burned with the light of science,
atomic clay mined from far-flung quarries
he shaped to molecules hard and round as marbles.
Those home-made mobiles revolved in outer space,
clear and cold, his clockwork constellations.

AT WILDE'S GRAVE

He is fixed in time, that boy
under the controversial angel.
His mother snaps him up
as so often before
into the black box at her hands.
The brother outside the wall
in cut-down denim scuffs his shoes.
He has new hair on his legs.
The gatekeeper who rings his bell
down the avenues of the dead
has refused him entry.
Their absent father is napping
in the back room of a posh suburb,
miles from this clear tolling.
He dreams of his sons' future.
It is closing time in Père Lachaise:
they've come to pay their respects.
A wild boy was Oscar, she puns,
turning to face her son
who leans against the stone.
Her cyclops lens loads and shuts.
He cannot go back or forward
so stands under that angel always.

DEAF MUTE

Now I can be vertical again
in this pink bedroom marooned by rain.
I orchestrate the loss repair
once more, lover, at my desk,
choosing my words carefully.
Among the papers I find your hairs,
black and straight, smelling of *gomina*.
It was such a perfect cut, falling
with cool abandon and style
like good ink brushes tracing hills
in Japanese washes, a bold outline
in the monsoon light.

The mirror casts an empty room
where my words fell on deaf ears.
I could explode and you would not hear,
preening your hair, using your fingers
to break the sound barrier,
to draw me within earshot.
Your remaining senses rallied to the cause,
sounding out, like me, the loss-repair.
You imagined growth where there was atrophy,
the silence suddenly filled with voices
speaking in tongues, your ears buzzing
with rumours from afar.

SILENT MOVIE

The volume stays at zero,
it's an old silent, a rerun
of one you've seen before.
The florid cards come up
at urgent moments: Help! Help!
Do you really love me?
— dubbed in your language.
The man behind the scenes
who mans the easel
is working overtime.
Our hero on the cliffedge
is hanging on for dear life.
His girl is thinking hearts
with words inside them.

A naked back is all I see
in the keyhole of the door
I'm banging to get in.
Behind me a shower drips.
You're deaf to all the world
and watch the film through
to the grande finale:
a silent tiger's roar
before cartoons and talkies.
You turn to shower off
the sweat I see
breaking on your back.
The towel falls to the floor
as you wonder where I've gone.

AFTER THE MOVIES

You go home to move your joystick
around the celestial junk
of inter-planetary disasters.
Your heroes are cunning men
in 3-D and boiler suits.
Those antennae on their brains
were built up bit by bit from science.

We've spent the wet afternoon
with another Spielberg offering,
a Hollywood Save the Children Fund
where the child is always right,
the carrier of mysteries, the monstrance.
His pretty face turns back the monster
built up bit by bit from method school.

I could almost believe it,
the clean *Bruderschaft*, King Kong
lifting the skinny orphans into light.
The new Boy Robins from Hollywood High
with boosters in their shoes
living out our Caucasian dream
on the rope bridge of good and evil.

It's a studio model, of course.
The star's location caravan
smells of Bourbon, that chest hair
peels off in the hands of the kid
whose mother pushed him this far
out into the rain, blinking like us,
our joysticks in our hands.

THE LOST WORDS

He turns the back issues
of *Time* cover to cover,
reading the pictures.
In infinite procession
they move away from him,
a comic-strip cartoon
of lives and faces
he knows and loves:
the lovely heroines
and sad disasters,
campaigns and wars,
fads and fashions
which litter the bed
we lie upon.

In time he turns to tell
the story of his eyes.
And fingers shape
a tall fiction
the pictures made:
his do-it-yourself
world of sound
dubbed with silence,
created in his own image.
Together we edit
and dissect the true
from the false,
and gaze in wonder
from one to the other.

In his quiet elision
is the might-have-been
of history, the wars
not fought or won,
the bulls not taken
by the horns and slaughtered.
Straws grasped again
in a different manner.
Somewhere the music

goes on, the names echo
which never hurt him.
All the back-issues
of words he could master
pile up there and elude him.

GLOW

for Steven Van der Zwan

I kept an eggshell for years,
one you painted secretly
that Easter in your loft
with those Glow-Tip pens
which withstand the heat.
It nested in tissue paper,

a funny face mislaid
by clumsy removal men
and dropped on the stairs
when I wasn't looking.
Its colours faded, but inside
there were traces of yolk.

At night I dream of faces:
dead ones breaking open
into life, coloured pens
painting on fragile shell
the features of your smile
glowing for me in the dark.

THE LONG HAUL

That almost forgotten thing
straight out of childhood
your chain coming off
into the closed pedal-box
of an old Dutch bicycle
and all the way home
you grip the belt of my pants
as I yoke your weight
along the flat back roads
between Utrecht and Odijk.
You get heavier and heavier,
my carrier-boy, my brother,
as the light of evening
is dying into night.

LUCKY BAGS

Sometimes a texture like skin
slips through my fingers
or the stops and rattles
of one cheap whistle
pierce the tedium
with warbling notes.
Then again I know the feel
of that erratic compass
whose North is haywire
and the ball-bearing
circumventing always
a hole in the nose
is quicksilver and alive
and Made In Taiwan.

There is a man inside
who dances on my hand
with heat, a live show.
That one propeller
and the halved fuselage
never quite fly free
of their armatures,
and the spit, glazing
transfers of Rin-Tin-Tin
and The Lone Ranger,
bubbles the sherbet
in the corner of the bag
like quicklime, or my mouth
blowing up balloons.

YAMEOGO AT THE IRON CURTAIN

Yameogo from Upper Volta
(now Burkina Faso)
boogied at the Iron Curtain
— one hand on his hip,
in the other a new Sony
ghetto-blaster bought
in downtown Hannover.
Bob Marley cut the wind
towards the Eastern bloc,
filling the air waves
where guards in their snugs
kept each other cool
fraternal company.

In the middle distance
red Soviet tractors
ploughed the traces
into no-man's land,
strip farming to the last.
Yame cocked his hip
to the tribal beat
and turned the volume up
high as it would go.
The metal fences buzzed.
While crows scattered
far and wide, either way,
making their own music.

AN IMAGINARY LINE

Flowers of frost double-glaze
our semi-detached as I stare
beyond the Wicklow hills to where
the rock-stars' estates are manned
by ex-Angels in biker suits.
Their leather reflects the Celtic dark.

Across our big bed in Kimmage
you've drawn an imaginary line,
saying: here is East and West Berlin
and here is the dividing wall,
built when I was born, and you
infinite among the cosmic possible.

I wake to the thin eiderdown
flying high above our cold war
and images of détente: your feet
making incursions into no-man's land,
a *Mauerspringer* on the ball
and the hard outlines softening

into dawn, the frost all gone
overnight the way of all frost
and one lone streetlight stuttering,
refusing to go off, or on,
like someone down on the lines
between here and there, hesitating.

THE STAMP COLLECTOR

for Artorius Konraad Wevers

Your small pictures have serrated edges,
you hunt them down in unmarked cartons
where all their fluttery colour hides
and camoflages that one priceless rarity.
It floats in my bathroom sink with other
lesser pieces of the landscape, the ones
you swop willy-nilly on Avenue Matignon.

There you have them in sets and series:
stoic heroes, commemorative implosions
beached on towels across the chair-backs,
little landscapes thrown up here to dry.
You live for these bonsai herbariums,
their perfect borders battening down
our pruned history of the known world.

They curl up to your green fingers
which tend and turn, ministering
to the best of your miniatures.
Then like a lepidopterist you fix them.
Ogre in your worlds, avid collector
of paper signs, lover of the small:
we have all this in common.

AN ABANDONED COUNTRY

Places one imagines
looking back on

as though from the satellites
sent out to probe deep space

an echo-sounder
brought home news

of an abandoned country
clouded in mist

and marbled features
revolving fast as ours.

The cameras zoom in
at point-blank range

on creatures down there
cloning mere life,

decked out in the attributes
of self and future self,

entwined in the old dances
back to snare us.

A Munch-scape of fjiords
and swirling skies

where there are no terrors
for the kids brought up

to fill the wet woods
with tree houses

and imaginary armies.
Where the reservoirs

deep in the hills
are full to brimming

and the loved one
charged and electric

time after time surfaces
at the ends of runways

like a new terminal.
Beam me down there

alien auto-pilot,
across the light years

to the smell of rain
and lightning in the thunderheads.

MOVING BOOKS

for Derry Ó Sullivan

The irony is the weight
carried from landing to landing.

The child is too old
for us to be hauliers.

She walks on her own,
sure-footed in the attic,

a cool Grace Pool
to set the house ablaze.

Can't you hear her laugh?
— a mad one certainly.

Nothing but bother
from beginning to end,

our pet hazard, our muse.
All that chain-smoking

and then this inferno
of dog-eared boxes

bursting at the seams,
her kindling, her *brosna*.

When the crunch comes
she'll be cinders, and the weight

light as a feather
— a dark one surely —

the irony of her fate.

ADULT EDUCATION

It could have been the Big Study
and Tits Magee's feline form
rubbing the radiators, smarting
under our hard men's jibes.
The rain was there, and the clouds
massed and dark as Indian ink.
The grown men and women writing
their adult education exercises.
All the past tenses beyond them.
And me, the hard man *par excellence*,
conducting the score, an understudy
for Mr Chips with his fences up.
They were taking it out
on the forty-year old queer
with the glasses and the stutter
while the monsoon came down.
Young Törless all over again.

I listened to the thunder
and the voice under the years
making its mute litany:

Let them not discover me,
now or ever, the deans, the trainee
Gardaí, Magee the father of four.
Lead me to live out my days
out foreign, cultivating bananas
and other tropical fruits.
Let the weather be mild
and the past only a rumour
of rain on the leaves
wide and smooth as shovels.
Let the houseboys be young
and reliable as prefects
patrolling the paths, spitting
betel juice into the undergrowth.
And me cool and snug as a Nazi
in that prayed-for enclave,
writing my memoirs.

MARTIN

I found him in an institution
at the back of the North wind.

He was locked in time, bearded,
older than his years even then.

It was the coldest winter
in Europe since records began:

farmers frozen in their fields;
packs of wolves in Czechoslovakia

down from the mountains for food.
He was warm against the heaters

with his fund of dirty pictures
and the idiotic laugh, muffled

from the back of the class.
Martin, good at spelling bees,

his snow-white baby's hair
and enormous hands and legs,

was kept back for years.
Now he's there forever.

CHILLIES

A skillet of chillies
laid out in the sun to dry,
incandescent, red,
candid to their crinkled tips.

Once my heart too
lay out there on fire,
incarnadine and raw,
careless of the noonday heat.

Until I took it in
to pound between the kern stones
of time and cruel irony,
and high in a cool pantry

packed a spice box
with sage and mint,
capers and savoury,
and the dust of all that sun.

TRAM IN THE YARD

The conductor-rod probes the sky
for lines. Once electricity
coursed down it, as now the rain
in runnels to the weather-proofed roof.
My tram is tethered to the ground
by gas, and all the empties
line up outside like Daleks.
The wheels have been derailed
and must go round in dreams
in a San Francisco of the mind,
riding nowhere fast. The grass
too has gone to seed, bamboo
and a small guava thicket
threaten to encroach this thing
— not a caravan, no longer a car
and too big to be a Tardis.
But out of time and place
it takes up space in my back yard,
late for me to play in,
small to inhabit, an omnibus
gone down one siding too many
and waiting in the rain
for signals, the go-ahead of current.

THE VOYEUR

The mosquito coil
makes a Celtic rune
on the teak floorboards.
There are others
paling into wood,
marking night vigils,
the slow round
of ash. Incense
above its sigla
keeps the Blitz at bay.

This Chinese hotel
behind the market
is riddled with holes.
My nightlight is off
the better to see
the young dreamer.
Dawn captures the sky.
We turn in on ourselves,
flame and aureole
burning at both ends.

IN THE BONSAI GARDEN

I dreamed of growing up
but every branch I grew
was thwarted, tampered with.
Now there's no going back.

I was contrary, and he
was there at every turn
turning me in on myself,
having his way with me.

Never a dull moment:
the braces, his funny corsets,
keeping me on my pins,
keeping me in the dark.

When I put out shoots
he'd want to know where
I was going, if I'd ever stop
playing around with myself.

I had no privacy.
Cut down to size,
stunted from the ground up,
a freak in his image.

Now I'm in my prime
he's after smaller fry
and puts me on display.
I can get up to no harm.

But overnight I dream
of flowers and fruit ripening
to a sticky fall.
A nightmare of sorts.

THE UNDERGROUND CITY AT KAYMAKLI

Eight floors underground
and still chipping
my living space
out of soft rock.

It is better than being stoned
by the thundering Muslim
in the overground —
there where I remember once
a warm sun and the tethered animals.

My caverns and passages
are mined with light
no heretic knows.
This flame feeds on chimneyed air.

When they come to get me
I will block the passages.
My dark anchorite's cell
will become tumulus.
I will burrow deeper to safety.

SNAP!

Me and you there
in the passage grave
looking cold
and overdressed

in windcheaters
and college scarves,
coloured the same
as that flash-lit

striated shale
bowling us over.
It will bury us
eventually,

and beside me
in place of you
the high priests
will lay these snaps

for the equinox
down that timeless
narrow passage
to happen on.

AHMED

He would light out
stealthily to the roof.
Naked and half-awake
I would watch him
from my dormer window,
narrow as jalousies
and open to the stars.
From the five minarets
of the pentapolis
prayer rained down
across our valley,
calling the faithful
to its own sweet music.
With the dawn he was in
again, up against me
and cleansed for love.

Hearing it once more
at his empire's end —
the same call and echo
from the far mosques
rattling my windows,
a teal-blue dawn rising
hours before it reaches
his walled settlements,
I wonder through what crack
he has found a way
to conjure life's rewards,
on what rooftop
has he bent and prayed
these eight short years
out among the stars,
and under whose gaze?

BOOTS

Exploring the loft again
I found his Civil Defence boots.
My half-hearted bovver brother
wore them in '74, blackening
the tiles of our *dacha*
in middle-class Outer Mongolia.

Before that I dangled
in free space, spurning
the top rung of the ladder
for miles of duckboards,
the wiring of the house
intricate as coded writing,

and the tank of well water
flush with a bobbing ballcock.
I tried my father's boots for size,
and, back to the cistern,
scanned his pamphlets for news.
What to do in time of war?

'Find the safest room in the house,
lay in a store of canned food,
candles, bandages, water.
Books may be useful, games
occupy the children.
Be prepared to stay in there

for a long time. Be ready
for any eventuality.
Fall-out is extremely dangerous;
it manifests itself
as blanket heat, unbearable
nearest the epicentre.'

I swung back down to ground level,
a good deal closer now.
The central heating purred.
Perhaps it's time to take them out
again. To polish the toes
and grease the stiffened tongues.

ELEMENTS

All that long hot Indian summer
we made an inventory of apparatus.
You in your brown chemist's coat
holed with acid, and my short pants
seeing out the end of childhood.

Strontium 90: the weight of a feather
on brand-new electronic scales.
Our lives in the fragile balance.
You were just turned fifty
and I was eleven years old.

You wrote the elements down
in a spidery, florid hand
with more than a hint of hurry.
Gaelic a's, the t's Caroline miniscule
on the long white ledger page.

Gold, silver, copper, zinc;
pure and uncompounded.
Alloys for weapons and tools.
X- and gamma rays
in their Pandora's boxes.

How could I ever want to know
the real weight of the world
or the elusive element of time?
In the inventory of that summer
they're hidden between the lines.

THE AMBASSADORS (after Holbein)

for Matthew Sweeney

Around us is the clutter
of our life and times:
torture instruments mostly,
thumbscrew and rack
and the subtler mechanisms
trailing wires in different colours.
Here too our swag bags,
marked SWAG in bright red,
spilling diamonds, bodies,
and invisible to the naked eye
the smaller chips and bits
which keep the state apparatus
more or less going.

It is not permitted
to look behind us
to the vanishing point.
But once he hung a mirror
on the wall opposite
(by accident or design?)
affording us a view.
There was a winding road
lined with travellers
such as us; diplomatic,
aware of their station,
not looking into the ditches
where the corpses lay.

Were they following us?
Was this mirror a conspiracy
of silence, and the houses
were they burning really,
or was it a trick of light?
Like always he has painted
fancy work in the margins.
Like him we try to imagine
an ideal landscape hidden there,
our bag of new toys spilling

contraptions with many sides,
mere instruments of measure,
the conundrums of space.

But instead, out of sight,
is this ghoulish image
we are disfigured with.
We alone cannot see it
from our angle.

RUE NATIONALE

I used to live doors away
from the Renault factory
at Boulogne-Billancourt.
Our flat overlooked Meudon,
where old man Céline lived.
Four floors of polish —
or was it three; the last
the years' embellishment?
A floor of memory.

You showed me a picture once;
Sartre on the rainbarrels
of *engagé soixante-huit,*
and under him the workers
outside the car factory
hanging on his every word.
His eye off to one side,
like us, years away, climbing
flights of polished stairs.

Other pictures I found myself,
and your nursery toys
put away for keepsakes
in the bottom drawers.
The little skull-caps
wrapped in tissue, and far back
a silver cup and candelabrum
like the family albums
hoarded from view.

My room contained the 'forties
and heady 'fifties, dresses
your mother wore, pill-box hats,
slim chain handbags whose sequins
captured the surrounding light
and threw it back to us.
Old Hebraic brooches put by
in cotton nest boxes
which fitted them exactly.

So onto this we added
a nest of our own. Filled,
Escher-like the floors grew
directions never planned,
the rooms so out of bounds
only imagination saw them.
Then the winds of change,
remember? All of Proust
lined on the piano lid

in the old Gallimard brown
— the cracked *papier calque* —
and most of it unread.
The big unkempt bed, and time
catching up with us at last.
The death of Sartre,
the streets to Montparnasse
lined with workers, *solidaire*,
pulling through on their own.

THE GYM TEACHER

I came across him in an ante-room
smoking a slim cigar. The near-effete
mannerism of his dying fall
performed lovely arabesques in the dark.

He was first up, shadow-boxing the hours
into light, jogging on the lakeside path.
Or Commanche-style in a ring, the one
pep-talking the boys, man to man.

For he was me in an afterlife
or one that came before, managed so well
only drink could break him, slowly over
the years learning the body's limits.

I could grow only to become him
and his flawed decay, and know that war,
like the whistle on his running suit,
is his friend for life. And thousands

like him, hard sane men ready to fight
the good fight. Stubbing their slim cigars
after lights-out in the dormitory,
yards from where the toned muscles sing.

ICE

I

Behind the sound of rain
the sound of ice. At night

the bent barbers shave
its glassy surface clean,

or, embroiled in cogs,
the blocks rumble dully

like impending glaciers
to come out cubes:

a loosened load
of transparent dice.

II

Remember the tipped-up
lens the rainbarrel's

exact collet made
to measure, the comeuppance

of soft water
for winter baths.

And lifting it out
intact as solid geometry

and cold as ... ice,
a plane surface newly glazed

and circumscribed
melting on the grass.

III

Wrist-deep in rainwater
my red hands plunge

the sawdusted ice.
Elementary immersions

harden selves to glass.
Learn to salvage

the melt water,
(seeing through one

to fathom the other).
To know solid ground

from quicksilver,
to play with the light

like mercury, running
messages for the gods.

GLIMMERS

It grows over
but then there are glimmers
still
the passage of light
to Granny's well.

A soundtrack joins
the original score of music:
shrill
unbroken voices
with big buckets

pulling back parabolas
of wild briar and tall nettles
down
to the clear water
welling up inside.

Our coign in sight
the buckets clatter and sink.
They're sinking still
as light flows over
and the glimmers fill.

THE SOURCE

There they were, fine
as dream could make them,
damming the stream.

Filigreed with light
filtered through trees
from no earthly source,

they played with water.
All day until night
its source was charted,

running through hands
so close to the well
its cold was sheer delight.

One was knee-deep
at the font, clearing
the tufted grass,

and further down-
stream, the other
carted boulders clear

for makeshift banks.
The third knew no bounds,
half in and out

of the swift current
their play had made,
manning the horizon.

Watch them there buoyant
in the stream, gathering
no moss. Already

one dead long before
he crossed the open sea.
And the others still

wondering beside
the dried-up pool
where the source had gone.

FREDDY

His back is to us
going out across ice.
An elusive puck
holds his attention
and the blurred
hockey-stick gripped
tight almost topples
his hard-won balance.
The weak light is failing.
Blue shadows abound
and form the wave
of scumbled snow
at the edge of the picture.
It is a Northern scene.
The boiler-suit is blue
and the wool jumper
down which its loose straps
fall, is bright yellow,
soaked through
to skin and bone.
A spark ignites
the cleared-back rink
where the skate blade
touches scored ice.
It appears steady, alive,
like the poised wave
and the playing child.

SWIMMING

i.m. Andrew Nelson

We swam so far out
the land was all antennas

and if someone waved
small wonder if we saw.

Far beyond the rock
we'd made out target

imagined trawlers
netted certain catch,

species fathom-deep
scuttled for cover,

snag-toothed, indifferent,
not anxious for news.

Treading water
to spite them,

or breasting alongside
its ebb and tow

we made it to that rock
and back again

to flop out on the sand.
The familiar sounds —

hawkers at their trade,
sandcastles subsiding,

some child's seaside day
destroyed by a row —

burst our muffled drums
and so implode there

forever. What lines
can stretch as far?

Now you're swimming out
again, insistent,

stroke for stroke,
steady us as you go.

THE VOYAGE OUT

He is leaning far back
to impress her. Starboard
and leeward the men ogle
her newfangled camera.

They are decked out in tweed
like early Jack B. Yeats.
He alone is bareheaded
and dressed in cool linen

hitched above the waistline
by braces. In the small lens
the buttons gleam, catching
the last rays of sea light.

A wonder it came out,
with the sun pulsing
far down in the background
and the waves upsetting

the angle of vision:
what, surely, it's all about.
For behind them, out of sight,
is Glengariff and the South,

and closer, the basalt
facets nudging elbow room
on the Giants' Causeway,
a plane surface on all sides.

Laid low down in the helm,
somewhere between Rockall
and freefall, I bide my time.
I too fit the picture,

miniscule and beside them.
And this is the voyage out,
crystal clear and brand new
and all of us large as life.

PLACES

GIDE'S SCISSORS

Tuck and fold time's drop stitches
neatly hem his pants
the well-tailored boy bewitches
summer's visiting aunts.

Though he climbs the dunes so nimble
and learns the rules real quick
wear him like a thimble
thread his needle with a lick.

What's that clinking in his pocket?
Who owns the Walkman in his pack?
Watch your camera or he'll hock it
while you're dreaming in the sack.

Lock your travellers in reception
hold on to those designer jeans
sex-tourism is all deception
that charmer's never what he seems.

O André in S.E.Asia's light,
O Willy in Tangier's glow,
these bum boys are all the same
fifty or a hundred years ago.

IN THE DESERT

There was one place in the desert
where I holed up for three days.
I still have visions.
Its 4-star hotel the Sahara Palace,
lost in the dunes. A convention
of holograph technicians
whipping it up by the pool.
They hardly ever came down
to my part of town.

I was the local hitcher
at the crossroads, tanning
my thumb. The young bloods
kept me company, and at night
talked of fucky-fucky in the datepalms
for a few dirhams. I stayed put,
and in the Hotel Fata Morgana
read till the one bulb sizzled
for next to nothing.

My fellow guest was a Ph.D.
in Sociology, down from the city
to get his facts straight, juggling
statistics in the foyer
till the dromedaries came home.
Through thin walls I heard
his heavy breathing and the flick
of magazines. I thought my bus
would never come.

Each day a vendor's stall
unfolded like a circus table
outside the school. Selling sweets
and sherbet twisted in old newspaper.
The kids queued in the glare
for lucky bags with transfers.
The days fizzled out at one.
When my bus came I didn't look back.
I still have visions.

SALVATORE (after Cavafy)

It was autumn and the scirocco was blowing.
You had a monkey hat and three scarves
because of the cold. I remember the braziers
of the chestnut vendors as they smoked
on the square, and afterwards
coffee and chasers at a zinc counter
in the Piazza della Nuovo Mundi.
You were thirteen going on fourteen.

I was in a *pensione* by the station
reading Dante's Inferno and Maigret mysteries.
All night the sky was bright with fire
where Etna rumbled, and this scarfe
left like a plume of smoke among the ash
of court and spark, kept me from the cold.
I was nineteen going on twenty.

IN THE ATLAS

Some of the oldest peaks
on Earth. We went up
at an angle, gunning the engines.
Millenia in the rearview mirror:
stacked and carbon-dated strata.
The weak sleet gave way
to flocks of thicker snow.
The villages thinned out.

At Medina, anytown, we cut the engines.
Silence all around.
Figures in cowled bournouses
tamped the drifting snow,
hopped up against the elements.
We had hours to wait —
a warm meal, fingers of tea —
until the first bus out of there.

In the one café I drew Europe
on the table's condensation.
Dribbled out my watery island
to the West, not unlike
these Spartan elevations:
cold to the marrow, cut off,
men doffing their hoods
in the mosque's sanctum,

and going about the business
of lynchpins and towropes,
axlegrease and hasps.
Riding in from hillside farms
for goods, a week's groceries,
dye for sheep and dye for hair
and toys for the youngsters
gadding in the outhouses.

. . . .

Coming down the other side
we passed the Camus farm,
ruined, off the roadside.
The far reaches lost in mist.
Boys flagged down our bus
with glittering aluminium cans.
Our ears unplugged and hoods
came clear as we approached the sea.

He could have been any one of them,
doing wee jobs, running up credit
in the Central Store, or standing
one foot higher than the other
at the side of that mountain,
not knowing which end of him was up.
A Titan of these hills, sniffing
sea-level, the heavens at his back.

FLYING EAST

The night I flew East
along the Tropic of Cancer
the boy in the bubble died.
Below me the lit runways
knitted sky and earth.
We swung up and away.
My hostess brought the papers
with yesterday's news
and tomorrow's deadlines
in all the known languages.
I was fed and wined,
the demonstration masks
came down, sure as eggs
is eggs, and this thin air
our fragile element.
Out there the northern lights
banked against cloud,
the pressure in our pod
climbed to new heights
of angst and adjustment.
Our seats slipped into recline.

PALE COUNTIES

i.m. Cathal Rooney

It never gets dark here,
there are always lines of light
— the dual carriageway, a city
over the horizon whose glow
orients us. But one night
we drove North through fog
in a grey landscape,

our pencil lights
startling the horses awake
at the white fences, picking out
finger posts and follies,
estates and walls, streams
murmuring from underground
watersheds, hopelessly lost.

Until we found our way
again, at 3 a.m., the dark
deepening as the dawn came,
and I remembered driving North
in just such a landscape,
us with our magic slates
to pass the time, sketching, erasing.

When we reached the white hospital
you had minutes to live
and no time to lose.
I am standing there again
with the machines ranged round
and their pale screens blank,
all the lines rubbed out.

A SUPPLEMENT TO THE
AMERICAN-VIETNAMESE
DICTIONARY

Under the A's we have:
acid trip, affluent society,
aureomycin (the latter
plugged my ears in '66).
We also have 4 entries
whose root is atom.
Ashram seems atmospheric,
followed by a hive of plosive B's:
barbed wire; battle fatigue; beautician.
Black humor begins to infiltrate.

The words start to conspire
among themselves:
bodycount, bomber, boner,
bra-less bisexual biker.
The enemy is language;
(underground in the bunkers)
it has perfect camouflage.
But where are the bodybags?
Curious omission.
Perhaps decency forbids.

The C's clot and cling
with a clued-in ring:
contraceptive, consciousness-
raising, cooperative,
cop-out (verb)/cop-out (noun).
Notice how the hyphens —
bridges on a make-shift map —
are here today, gone tomorrow.
They round off with
crematory, crunch.

After that words double-talk;
enemy aliens, surrealistic
cluster-bombs in the dark:
dictaphone, dictatorship,
dinette, discotheque.
Like hippy(ie) hallucinants
they echo a long time under you
(mine sweeper; mind-expanding)
or lift you off your feet:
paramedic; paranoia; peanut butter.

Under U the laylines
show thru' (You-whoo!):
Uncle Tom, underdeveloped,
underdog, underground,
but end on a positive note:
upkeep and utopian.
(Ultimatum and umpty-umpth
are in there too).
V has veni, V.D.
and vital statistics.

The W's are washed-up
war-mongers, wise-
cracking white collar
workers whose wives
are wage-earning
Women's Liberationists
(with washing machines).

By itself in a corner
 a solo performer
  xenophobia.

NIGHTDRIVE NEAR CAMBODIA

Elephants at the saltlick
just outside our torches'
vacillating range. And deer
coming down nervous at night
into the jungle clearings.

Out where the one light was stars
we broke cover and drove, spying
Halley's comet between two wires,
taut as if their ends were poles
apart, and the Earth finite.

For a moment the glow
of that far, Viconian traveller
caught fire and went round
our loose, soon split-apart circle.
It was time to turn and go.

. . . .

Driving back to camp
I thought of those cables
twanging twenty years of war
around the world. Of the kids
we'd bedded down in undergrowth

whose daddies ranged these hills
like comets in their might,
a distant fire show trailing
twenty years of sparks and ash.
Left and right of that road

the jungle dark went on.
The batteries in our torches
ran down. And the nervous deer
wearing away the saltlicks
stayed clear of our lights.